SPACE PIRATES

Treasure!

JIM LADD

Illustrated by
Benji Davies

nosy
crow

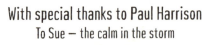

With special thanks to Paul Harrison
To Sue — the calm in the storm

First published in the UK in 2014 by Nosy Crow Ltd,
The Crow's Nest, 10a Lant Street, London SE1 1QR, UK

Nosy Crow and associated logos are trademarks and/or registered
trademarks of Nosy Crow Ltd

Text © Hothouse Fiction, 2014

Illustrations © Benji Davies, 2014

The right of Hothouse Fiction to be identified as the author of this work
has been asserted by them in accordance with the Copyright, Designs and
Patents Act, 1988

Printed and bound in the UK by Clays Ltd, St Ives Plc

Papers used by Nosy Crow are made from wood grown in sustainable forests.

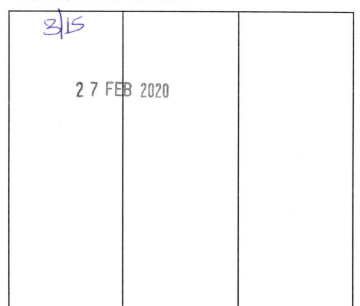

Look out for more
stories of swashbuckling
space adventures in

Stowaway!

Stranded!

Mutiny!

Who's who in COMET'S CREW

CAPTAIN COMET

SAM STARBUCK

PEGG AND LEGG

BARNEY

Who's who in BLACK-HOLE BEARD'S CREW

BAGGOT

YARR

BLACK-HOLE BEARD

Chapter One
BREAKFAST AND WORMHOLES

SPACE PIRATES

Samson Starbuck stood in the crow's nest of the pirate spaceship the *Jolly Apollo*. He looked out at the Universe all around him. The deep black of space was scattered with colourful clouds of gas, the short, bright tail of a fast-moving purple comet and countless pinpricks of light. Sam knew that each one of those lights was a star, and each of those stars could be surrounded by planets. And on one of those planets his parents were space-shipwrecked and waiting to be rescued.

Sam turned his attention to the tattered piece of cloth in his hand. It was a rough map that his mum had scribbled on a scrap of spacesuit material. She had sent it to Sam in their ship's homing beacon. It showed the way to the planet where his parents' spaceship had crashed while they'd been scouring the galaxies for new forms of plant life.

Luckily, they had landed on Planet X, which space-pirate legend claimed was a famous treasure planet, with islands of rubies. Sam's only hope of rescuing his parents had been to stow away on

Treasure!

a space-pirate ship. When the pirates found out that Sam had a map to the legendary Planet X, they were happy to let him join the crew.

As Sam had discovered, choosing the *Apollo* was both the best *and* worst decision he could have made. The crew were terrible at being pirates: they were always getting lost, they never found any treasure, they argued with each other and the food on board was terrible. However, they were also kind-hearted, loved a good space-shanty, enjoyed a game of ten-pin bowling (all space-pirate ships had at least one bowling alley on board), and always looked out for each other – including Sam, who was now the cabin boy.

"Korraaaackkkkkk! Korraaaackkkkkk!"

An indescribable sound battered the silence of Sam's lookout post.

"Korraaaackkkkkk! Korraaaackkkkkk!"

The deafening screech rattled around the *Apollo* again. Sam groaned. The noise was coming from a Pgtargan cockerel, the noisiest type of bird in the tri-galaxy network. Captain Comet had bought it

3

at the last space port. He thought the crew needed
something to get them up in the mornings, which
was probably true, but the cockerel had swiftly
become the least popular thing on board the ship.
In fact, it was probably the least popular thing
to ever have been on *any* space-pirate ship, and
that was saying something. Even from up high in
the crow's nest Sam could hear the curses of his
fellow shipmates.

Treasure!

But it wasn't the only noise Sam could hear – there was also the unmistakable sound of someone climbing the rigging to the crow's nest. And, given the awful smell wafting upwards, it had to be Barney, the ship's cook, with breakfast.

A large tentacle curled over the edge of the rail and moments later Barney hauled himself up next to Sam. It was a bit of a tight squeeze in the crow's nest as Barney was a huge multi-tentacled Kraken. He looked truly terrifying, but Barney was actually the gentlest soul on board the *Apollo*, and Sam's best friend on the ship.

"Morning, Sam. I knew you were on lookout duty so I thought I'd bring you breakfast in the nest," said Barney with a smile.

Sam looked at the plate Barney was clutching in one of his tentacles. Two lumpy eggs squatted in a green slime, like toads in a swamp. It looked like there were hairs sprouting from the top of the bluey-white shells.

"They're Gnarf eggs!" said Barney proudly. "I've been saving them since we left P-Sezov 8.

They should be good and ripe by now – just the way the people of Gnarf eat them!"

"Aren't the people from Gnarf famous for having no eyes and zero sense of taste or smell?" asked Sam.

"That's right!" said Barney delightedly. "Anyway, spotted anything interesting?"

"Yeah, look at that!" said Sam, pointing ahead of them. As well as the bright-purple comet streaking towards them and the glow from the surrounding stars, there was a strange glowing circle of light, easily as bright as a sun. Inside it, multicoloured lights throbbed and flashed.

"That's got to be this bit," said Sam, pointing to the map excitedly. "Which means we're pretty close to Planet X! What is that thing, anyway?"

"That'll be the Lightning-Bolt Wormhole. I haven't seen it before, but I've heard about it," Barney replied. "See those coloured lights? They're pulses of energy."

"Wow!" said Sam. "It looks like we could cut through the wormhole, which would get us to

Planet X even quicker!"

Sam noticed that Barney wasn't looking quite so excited at that thought.

"I'm not sure that's a great idea," said Barney.

"Why?" asked Sam.

"The Lightning-Bolt Wormhole is famous. Famously *deadly*. No one's ever made it all the way though. Some people have tried to fly though it, surfing on the energy waves. They call it 'riding the lightning'," Barney told him. "In fact, Mad Jack McGee did it... I was at his funeral."

"Funeral?" asked Sam.

"Oh yeah. He got most of the way through but he got a *bit* disintegrated towards the end. Lovely sandwiches they had after the funeral."

Barney smiled at the memory.

"What happened?" asked Sam.

"Well, I had three of the Steiffell shrimp sandwiches and a handful of those little sausage things..." Barney noticed Sam's face. "Oh, you mean how did he die? Well, the wormhole is

7

full of lightning," Barney explained. "If one of those bolts hits your ship while you're riding a wave then you're toast."

"And how likely are you to get hit?" asked Sam.

"See for yourself," Barney replied, pointing at the wormhole. "No one's ever gone into the Lightning-Bolt Wormhole and come out to tell the tale. That's all that's left of those that have tried."

Barney pointed a tentacle at the wormhole. Sam squinted and could just make out the wreckage of battered and scorched spaceships floating around the wormhole.

"Oh…" said Sam.

"Oh, don't worry," said Barney, putting a comforting tentacle on Sam's shoulder and pointing at the

map with another. "Look, if we go around the wormhole it'll be fine. I'm sure a small detour won't take too much longer."

Sam looked at the map.

"Well, we need to fly through the Grey Star Belt in that case," said Sam. "It's a longer route than going though the wormhole, but it'll be safer. And I'm sure it won't be *too* boring."

Barney didn't say anything.

"Oh, Barney, please tell me it's not boring," Sam pleaded.

"Anyway, I'd better be getting on with the crew's breakfast," said Barney quickly. "I'll just leave your Gnarf eggs here."

Barney scrambled back down the main mast, leaving Sam alone.

"Great," he muttered. "We don't get to ride the lightning *and* we have to spend more time going through some boring star belt instead!"

He slumped against the rails and watched the giant forks of lightning flickering around the wormhole's entrance, and the bright, colourful flashes of the energy waves coming from within. Sam stared at the pulsing light and swayed to a gentle swishing sound. His eyes felt heavy and he yawned widely, lulled by the back-and-forth of the soft sound. Suddenly his eyes burst open – *swishing sound*? Where was that noise coming from?

Sam peered over the edge of the crow's nest and looked around hurriedly. A ship was edging out from behind the purple comet Sam had seen earlier. The noise was the sound of oars being pulled through the air as a horde of space pirates tried to sneak up on the *Jolly Apollo*! Sam immediately recognised the menacing lines of the large, dark vessel that was edging towards them and his heart fell. It was the *Gravity's Revenge*!

Chapter Two

ALERT! ALERT!

Treasure!

For a moment Sam froze. The *Gravity's Revenge* was under the command of Black-Hole Beard, the most fearsome pirate in the known universe. He was a giant of a man and everything about him was angry: an angry scowl; evil, angry eyes; even his hair and bushy beard were wild and fierce-looking. But what Black-Hole Beard was most angry about was the fact that Sam had the map to Planet X, the universe's greatest treasure hoard, and he didn't.

Black-Hole Beard had tried lots of ways to get his hands on the treasure map, and now Sam was sure he was about to try again.

Sam hit a big red button on the mast and the emergency siren started to wail. Seconds later the crew blundered on to the deck, half asleep, pulling on their clothes and doing up their buttons wrong. The pirates of the *Jolly Apollo* were used to panicking, but the warning siren meant it was something serious, and that resulted in *serious* panicking. The space sailors dashed this way and that, pulling on their clothes, hopping about as

13

they tried hitching up their trousers, bumping into each other and falling over.

"It's Black-Hole Beard!" Sam yelled down, but no one could hear him over the noise of the siren and the confusion on the deck.

Sam swung over the rails of the crow's nest and scrambled down the rigging two rungs at a time. When he got halfway he leapt from the ropes and slid down the main mast like it was a fireman's pole. He landed on the deck just as Captain Comet appeared from his cabin. He was still in his pyjamas, which had a skull-and-laser-cutlasses pattern on, and was sleepily clutching a soft toy Kraken. Comet yawned, stretched extravagantly, and looked round blearily with the only one of his three eyes that wasn't covered by an eye patch.

"What's going on, Sam? My moustache was twitching so much it woke me up. And you know what a twitchy 'tache means – there's trouble afoot!"

"Hang on, your moustache woke you up, not

14

the siren?" Sam was dumbfounded.

"Pardon?" Comet asked, leaning towards Sam and pulling an earplug out of his ear. "Sorry, didn't catch a word of that. I sleep with these in now to block out that cockerel's awful squawking— SAM, THE WARNING SIREN IS GOING OFF!"

"I know! Look!" Sam pointed to the *Gravity's Revenge*.

"Aaarrrgghh!" screamed Comet, staggering about dramatically. "Oh dear! I don't feel too well…"

"Yep, I was expecting that," Sam said to himself. "Pegg! Legg!" he shouted to the two-headed first mate. "It's Black-Hole Beard! We need to get out of here – fast!"

Comet clutched his teddy bear to his chest. Sam could practically hear the cogs in his mind grinding into gear.

"Man the main anchor! Haul the sail! Boosters to full speed and hard to starport, no, portboard, no, I mean turn *right*!" babbled Comet at his crew.

Pegg and Legg ran to the ship's wheel.

Suddenly a panicked look came into the captain's eye. "Quick, Sam, take this," Comet said, fishing a key on a chain from around his neck. "It's the key to the grum store. You have to lock it before Black-Hole Beard gets here!"

Sam knew that foamy, lemon-flavoured grum was a space pirate's favourite drink, and he knew how upset Comet had been last time Black-Hole Beard had stolen their supplies, but surely that wasn't the most important thing to worry about right now? "But, Captain—" he started, but Comet waved him away.

"The grum, Sam, protect the grum!" he flapped wildly. "There's not a moment to lose!"

Sam sighed and raced across the deck, weaving in and out of groups of confused pirates as he went. He ran down the steps to the lower deck, past the bowling lanes, into the kitchen and BANG – straight into a huge tray of Gnarf eggs that were sitting on the worktop. The tray flew into the air and the greasy cooked eggs landed on the floor with a SPLAT.

Sam looked at the mess guiltily, but there was no time to stop. He sped off to the grum store, locked the door, stuffed the key in his pocket and charged back to the deck. When he got back, things were looking just as chaotic as before. Pegg and Legg were arguing with each other about which way to turn the wheel, and the sails were going up and down as Comet barked conflicting orders. Sam turned to see how close the *Revenge* was when he was blinded suddenly

by a bright-red light.

"What's that?" Sam shouted.

He shielded his eyes and watched as six red lights stretched from the *Revenge* to the *Apollo*. The beams were thick and looked like glowing elastic – it was as if the two ships were joined by great grasping tentacles of luminous red rubber.

"Traction beams," Comet gasped.

"I thought traction beams were a myth," said Piole, the twelve-mouthed crew member, as he looked over the side

at the red beams.

"Evidently not," Comet replied, nervously.

The traction beams attached to the side of the ship with a *twang*, pulling the *Jolly Apollo* next to the *Gravity's Revenge*. Captain Black-Hole Beard leaned nonchalantly against the rails of his ship and glared at the *Apollo*. Behind him skulked his brother, Goldstar. Goldstar also wanted to get even with Sam and Captain Comet. He'd tried and failed to commandeer the *Jolly Apollo* and the crew had abandoned him on an asteroid in just his pants!

"Why, good morning, Joseph," Black-Hole Beard shouted to Comet. "I thought I'd pop by to show you my new toys." He gestured to the traction beams. "I 'borrowed' these from a Stovian Science Ship and blow me down if they don't work a treat!"

"What do you want?" Comet shouted as bravely as he could.

"You know what I want, Comet," Black-Hole Beard snapped. "Every time I steal that map, you meddlesome star-warts somehow get it back, so this time I'm not going to let you out of my sight. If you want to reach Planet X, you'll have to take us too, and these little beauties mean you can't run off without us. I'm sticking to you like a barnacle on a moonwhale's backside. You're not getting away this time!"

Chapter Three
Escape

Insults and curses rained down on the *Jolly Apollo* from the crew of the *Revenge*.

"You've got the map, but we've got *you*, ya useless swabs!" cried a heavily tattooed pirate from Black-Hole Beard's ship.

"Tricking the *Apollo* is like taking candy from a baby: easy. And I *love* candy!" smirked One-Hand Luke, a stooped and particularly fearsome crew member with a hydraulic hook at the end of one arm.

"What now?" asked Sam, doing his best to ignore the insults.

"Let's get them off!" Pegg shouted. He and Legg leaned over the side of the *Jolly Apollo*, but before they could touch the nearest beam, Black-Hole Beard's crew released a volley of laser-cannon balls. Pegg and Legg leapt back, their stripy jumper looking a bit singed.

"Hands off the beams," Black-Hole Beard snarled. "First one of ye scurvy maggots that touches them will have fewer fingers left than One-Hand Luke here." One-Hand Luke gave an evil grin and waved his hydraulic hook menacingly.

"Right-ho, me hearties," said Comet. "Time for a quick crew meeting."

Everyone gathered round and did their best to ignore the salty scoffing from the ship opposite.

"Well, looking on the bright side, they haven't boarded us," said Comet.

"Yet!" grumbled Pegg, the grumpier of the first mate's two heads.

"Aye, you're right, shipmate," Comet agreed. "So we need to find some way of escaping from the *Revenge*. Any ideas, anyone?"

"How about we go in the wrong direction on purpose?" said Vulpus, the furriest of the pirates. "That way we fool Black-Hole Beard into

thinking Planet X is somewhere else."

"Yes, but we'll be going in the wrong direction too," said Romero, a scary-looking Snippernaut, who was like a giant walking lobster with two large pincers for hands. "And they'll still be attached to us."

Everyone thought hard and scratched their heads.

"What you all need is some breakfast – a bite to eat will get those grey cells working," said Barney, arriving on deck with trays of steaming food clutched in his tentacles. "You're in for a treat too, it's scrambled Gnarf eggs!"

Sam wasn't sure if anyone *really* thought this was a treat, but at least forcing down breakfast was a break from trying to think up a plan.

"Had to do some quick thinking there," said Barney, as he sat down next to Sam. "Some space maggot knocked the Gnarf eggs on to the dirty floor, so I had to scoop them all up and scramble them instead."

Oops, thought Sam guiltily.

24

Treasure!

"You OK, Sam? You look a bit funny," asked Barney. "Don't worry about the taste – to be honest, I think the dirt has improved things."

"It's not the eggs," Sam sighed (although it was partly the eggs), "it's Black-Hole Beard. We were well on our way to Planet X and now he comes along and ruins everything."

"Ha! Call that breakfast?" came a shout from the *Revenge*. A pirate was holding up a plate of food. "I wouldn't feed that to a meteor pig. *This* is a breakfast!"

"They've got grilled wafflous with beeloo syrup," whined Piole.

"And I can smell bacostring!" sighed Legg.

"And sweetrooms, and gnargleberry, and starywisps…" added Piole, drooling from all twelve of his mouths and making a puddle on the deck.

"How did you cook that slop? In a tumble drier?" mocked another pirate from the *Revenge*.

"Hmmph!" huffed Barney. "Of course their food's great; *their* chef is from the Michelin Star.

But my cooking's not bad, is it, Sam?"

Sam's mind raced. Barney's cooking was monumentally awful, but Sam couldn't say that to his friend.

"Erm, your cooking is … *unique*," said Sam.

"Unique?" Barney replied.

"Sure! There's no one that cooks like you, Barney," said Sam.

Barney's beak-like mouth cracked into a smile.

"I'm unique," he smiled, and wandered happily back to the kitchen.

"Right, me hearties. Your captain has a plan!" said Comet proudly as he called the crew back into a huddle – safe from the prying ears of the *Revenge*. "We fire up the engines full blast and see how strong those traction beams are. If we accelerate as quickly as we can I reckon we can break free. Now, I want all of you to get into position: Pegg and Legg take the wheel; Zlit, make sure those boosters are primed and ready to go. The rest of you get ready to drop those sails; we need as much power as we can get. We'll break free of those scurvy rogues, just see if we don't!"

"And don't let on we're up to anything," warned Sam. "Just act naturally."

Everyone took their positions; but as they tried to pretend everything was normal they went a bit over the top.

Sam groaned as he watched the pirates having loud, exaggerated chats about the weather and whistling space-shanties a bit too loudly.

Barney tried crossing his tentacles casually and ended up tying two of them together in a knot.

If anyone had been watching from the *Revenge* they would have suspected something was up right away. Luckily Black-Hole Beard's crew were too busy with their twelve-course breakfast to notice. Eventually the *Apollo*'s crew were in position. Zlit and Romero were helping to drop the sails, Jonjarama was making sure the gravity anchors were stowed properly, and Pegg and Legg were standing by the ship's wheel. Sam nodded at Comet, who gave a huge, exaggerated wink and drew his laser cutlass.

"Now!" shouted Comet dramatically, slicing his sword downwards through thin air. "Full speed ahead and let's break those traction beams!"

The *Apollo*'s engines roared into life and the sails dropped with a mighty flap. The ship creaked and groaned with the sudden acceleration, the ropes sang as they were stretched by the pull of the sails and the engines whined with the effort. Everything that wasn't fastened down shook and

28

rattled. Sam could feel his teeth chattering with the vibrations. It was one of the rare occasions that everyone was concentrating on their job.

Almost immediately, smoke began to billow from below, cloaking the *Apollo* in a choking black fog. Sam coughed and spluttered as he breathed it in.

"It's the engines, Captain," shouted Zlit through the thick smoke. "I think they're going to blow!"

"Ten more seconds, Mr Zlit," Comet cried. "Then we'll be far enough away from the *Revenge* to drop speed!"

The smoke on the deck was so thick that Sam could barely see his hand at the end of his arm. Those few seconds seemed to last an age as the engines shuddered with the effort.

"D-d-d-d-drop ... s-s-s-s-s-peed ... t-t-t-t-to ... c-c-c-cruise," ordered Comet's voice through the smoke, his words shaken out of him by the vibrations of the ship.

With a grateful sigh the engines eased off and

the ship stopped shaking.

"Well, that should have done it," came Comet's voice confidently.

The smoke slowly cleared, and revealed – *Gravity's Revenge*! The *Apollo* had moved precisely nowhere. The *Revenge* was still attached and the traction beams were as strong as ever.

"Are you going somewhere, Joseph?" called Black-Hole Beard as his crew laughed and jeered. "Yarr!" Black-Hole Beard called to the giant Minocerous who served as his first mate. "Let's teach these space-rats a lesson. Fire!"

Chapter Four
FULL SPEED AHEAD!

A crackle of laser blasts ripped across the *Apollo*'s deck. Sam jumped to one side as the deadly ball from a laser musket flew past and left a scorched black mark against the base of the main mast. Sam could hear One-Hand Luke laughing as he jumped up and down, firing manically. All over the deck, pirates dived for cover behind anything they could find: chests, barrels or, in Comet's case, behind Sam. The shooting stopped as abruptly as it had started.

"Let that be a warning to you!" bellowed Black-Hole Beard. "Try any more tricks, you scabby wretches, and I'll be firing the laser cannons instead!"

"Cawr!" croaked Baggot, the strange creature that sat on Black-Hole Beard's shoulder. It was covered in red feathers but had furry legs so it looked like a cross between a space-rat and a parrot. "Cawr! You'll be filled with more holes than Comet's socks."

Black-Hole Beard roared with laughter.

"Aye, you're right, Baggot," laughed the

Revenge's captain. "And it would be shame to ruin such a lovely pair of pyjamas!"

"Cawr!" crowed Baggot, before bursting into song:

"He talks nothing but flim-flam,
He's wearing his jim-jams,
His ship is
a rusty old boot,
It's Comet,
the useless
old coot!"

"I'd like to fire that furry monstrosity out of a laser cannon," muttered Comet, still flushed red with embarrassment.

"Why don't you go and get dressed, Captain," Sam suggested. "Then we'll try and think of a way to get rid of those traction beams."

Still muttering about Baggot, Captain Comet slunk below deck. He returned a couple of minutes later in his usual flamboyant clothes: a brightly coloured frock coat, a frilly shirt and his best breeches.

"I've got an idea," Sam told him.

"What? On how to get hold of Baggot?" asked Comet, looking keen.

"No, on how to get rid of Black-Hole Beard," Sam replied.

Comet looked disappointed, then perked up as he suddenly realised what Sam had said.

"Do tell," he said eagerly.

The crew gathered round to hear the new plan.

"Well, if we can't break away," said Sam, "and there's no way we can fight our way out of this—"

"There most certainly isn't," said Comet hurriedly.

"Then perhaps we can *scare* him away," Sam continued.

Treasure!

"Scare Black-Hole Beard? Are you mad? *Nothing* scares Black-Hole Beard!" gasped Legg.

"I bet going into the Lightning-Bolt Wormhole would," said Sam with a smile.

The crew gasped.

"You want to try going through the Lightning-Bolt Wormhole? You're mad!" said Pegg grumpily.

"Pegg's right, me hearty," said Comet. "It's certain doom. Just look at this."

Comet switched on the holoscreen on the main deck and brought up information on the Lightning-Bolt Wormhole.

He read out loud: "It is said that the Lightning-Bolt Wormhole has claimed one thousand, three hundred and twenty-three ships to date... No ship has proved that it is possible to pass through the wormhole... The lightning bolts are so powerful they can disable a ship's power, or in extreme cases actually blow a ship apart."

Somewhere amongst the silent crew someone gulped loudly.

"Trying to fly one ship through that wormhole is a suicide mission, but trying to do it with two ships joined together is … is … Well, it's just *silly*," concluded Comet.

"I'm not suggesting we *actually* go through it," Sam grinned at the crew. "We just make Black-Hole Beard *think* we're going to go through it. We'll scare him so much that he releases the traction beams. As soon as he lets us go we'll make a run for it and try to lose him in the Grey Star Belt."

"What's that, me hearty – a double cross? Arr, that's proper piratin', lad!" said Comet.

Sam smiled at the compliment.

"Right, me hearties," shouted Comet, "Let's get the *Apollo* ready to sail and I'll tell Black-Hole Beard we're off."

Sam was doubly pleased. He was happy that he'd come up with a plan to get them out of another sticky situation: but he was even happier that they'd be getting a better view of the Lightning-Bolt Wormhole. Even though he knew it was dangerous, he couldn't help feeling excited about the whirling vortex.

Pegg and Legg took the wheel, Vulpus climbed to the crow's nest, Romero and Zlit got ready to haul anchor and the rest of the crew busied themselves with the sails.

"Ahoy there, *Gravity's Revenge*," Comet called. "Prepare to sail. We're heading for Planet X."

"So you've seen sense at last, Comet," Black-Hole Beard replied. "Cawr! I doubt that, I doubt that!" added Baggot.

"Raise the anchor, One-Hand Luke!" Black-Hole Beard bellowed. "Yarr, take the wheel! That rusty old tub the *Apollo* is going to make us rich!"

Cheers rang out from the *Revenge* as she raised her gravity anchors and the crew manned her sails.

"Cruise speed, dead ahead, please," said Comet. The *Apollo*'s rocket boosters spluttered into life. Behind them the *Revenge* didn't bother firing their own boosters, relying on the *Apollo* to tow them to their destination. Sam watched the *Revenge*, eagerly waiting for the moment Black-Hole Beard would notice what was happening.

A few minutes later, Black-Hole Beard and his younger brother, Goldstar, suddenly rushed to the side of the *Revenge*'s deck rail, bellowing at the *Apollo*.

"Comet, you planet lubber!" Black-Hole Beard yelled so angrily that flecks of spit burst out of his mouth and collected in his beard. "You pestilent maggot! You Nungaloid nitwit!"

Treasure!

"Change course," Goldstar shouted. "You're headed straight for the wormhole!"

"I am aware of that," Comet replied coolly. "But I will not change course, for that *is* our course."

"Avast with this madness, Comet – it's certain doom!" shouted Black-Hole Beard.

Comet smiled haughtily and turned to Pegg and Legg. "Full speed ahead, me hearties, full speed ahead!"

Chapter Five

A DEATH TRAP

Treasure!

"Now now, stop this nonsense, Comet!" wheedled Goldstar. "Not even you'd be such a fool as to try to fly through the Lightning-Bolt Wormhole. It's a deathtrap!"

"I am and I will," said Comet. He thought for a moment. "Apart from that bit about being a fool."

The *Apollo*'s speed picked up until they were racing towards the wormhole.

"Turn off your traction beams, Black-Hole Beard," called Comet. "Then you can fly off to some *safe* bit of space."

"I've got a better idea, Captain *Calamity*," shouted Black-Hole Beard. "Your lightweight ship is no match for my *Revenge*. All I have to do is drop anchor and you'll come to a stop."

"Oh, I hadn't thought of that," muttered Comet to himself.

Sam watched nervously as Black-Hole Beard barked out an order. The *Revenge*'s gravity anchors came clanking down – but nothing happened.

Black-Hole Beard looked dumbfounded.

"Fire the rocket boosters! Reverse thrust!" he bellowed.

The *Revenge*'s engines roared into life, but instead of pulling the ships away from the wormhole, they kept on their course. Sam turned to Captain Comet, but he looked just as confused as Black-Hole Beard.

"Pegg, Legg, have you made any, er, *improvements* to the engines?" asked Comet.

"And when would we have done that?" replied Pegg. "They're just as useless as before."

"So what's going on? We shouldn't be able to pull the *Revenge* this easily. It's like we're fishing for Zimopan dwarf sprats with a megaton winch," said Comet.

"Oh, no!" said Sam, pointing to the holoscreen. "No, no, no, no! It says here that the wormhole has a gravitational pull."

"A what?" asked Comet. "*Gravitational pull? What does that mean?*"

"It means that if we get too close, the wormhole will suck us in!" said Sam.

Treasure!

"Pegg! Legg! Change course!" shouted Comet in a sudden panic.

"Where to, Captain?" asked Legg.

"I don't care!" Comet replied, pointing at the wormhole. "Just away from that!"

Pegg and Legg struggled with the ship's wheel, trying to turn it one way or another.

"We can't change course!" cried Legg. "No matter which way we turn the wheel we just keep going straight!"

"*What?* Do you mean we can't get away?" said Comet, horrified.

"I don't know, Captain, but we're headed for the Lightning-Bolt Wormhole!"

"We need to do something quickly," said Sam, "or it's going to be too late!"

"Switch the traction beams off," Comet shouted at the *Revenge*. "We might both be able to get away if the ships are separated."

It was Black-Hole Beard's turn to look panicked.

"I don't know how!" shouted Black-Hole

Beard. "We stole them, and we don't have the instruction manual! Curses! I knew we should have kidnapped one of the scientists too!"

"Cawr! Said scientists were a waste of space, you did," croaked Baggot. "No scientist belongs on the *Revenge,* that's what you said. CAWR!"

Black-Hole Beard grabbed Baggot off his shoulder and stuffed him head first into a laser cannon.

"Shut yer beak,
Baggot, or I'll fire you
off into space!" roared Black-Hole Beard.

Sam watched as Black-Hole Beard stormed off and left. Baggot wriggled his way out of the top of the cannon, feathers spewing everywhere, and stuck his tongue out at Black-Hole Beard's back.

"We'll get you for this, just you wait and see!" Goldstar yelled, flinging his cape over his shoulder dramatically and following his brother.

In front of them the wormhole spiralled menacingly, energy waves disappearing into it like water swirling down a plughole. Everything looked much larger now that they were getting closer, and the lightning flickered around the edges with a spine-chilling crackle.

KABOOM!

A laser-cannon shot exploded next to the *Apollo*.

"Comet!" shouted Black-Hole Beard. "What are you playing at? I don't know what you're up to or how you're doing it, but stop it now or I'll blow your ship to smithereens!"

"I can't help it!" wailed Comet. "It's the wormhole – it's sucking us in!"

"Blistering bowling balls! You've done it now, you fool!" bellowed Black-Hole Beard.

"Sam, go to the crow's nest and swap places

with Vulpus," ordered Comet, pulling himself together. "I'll want him down here to help with the sails. We're going to need all hands, tentacles and claws on deck if we're going to out-run the pull of the wormhole. You keep a look out up there. See if you can find any weak spots in the wormhole."

"Weak spots?" asked Sam.

"Oh, I don't know!" blustered Comet. "Just find us a way out of here!"

Sam scampered up the rigging to the crow's nest as fast as he could and passed on Comet's orders to Vulpus, the huge, furry crewmate.

From his vantage point on top of the main mast, Sam could see Comet dashing this way and that and shouting orders to everyone. The crew members ran around in confusion as they tried to turn Comet's orders into actions. Things weren't much better on the *Gravity's Revenge*.

Sam could see Black-Hole Beard frantically trying to find ways of shutting off the traction beams. He tried firing laser muskets at them,

but the blasts just bounced off. There were pirates desperately bashing the traction beams with oars and hoverpins.

All the while the ships were getting closer to the Lightning-Bolt Wormhole and the dreadful churning, crackling noise was getting louder and louder. In no time at all it was looming over the two ships in its full, terrible glory. Sam could see right inside the wormhole now, where waves of blue pulsing energy tumbled and spun into a long tunnel. The occasional bolt of lightning crackled and sparked out of the waves.

Sam shuddered. Just a few minutes before, he had been desperate for a close-up look of the wormhole; now he wanted to be anywhere else but here.

Soon, the entrance to the wormhole seemed to fill up the whole sky. Sam felt his stomach flip over as the two ships were dragged towards its churning mouth. The noise was now deafening; a relentless roar that made Sam's eardrums ache and his head feel like it was going to erupt.

Treasure!

"Grab something and hold on tight, me hearties!" shouted Comet against the roar of the wormhole. "We're going in!"

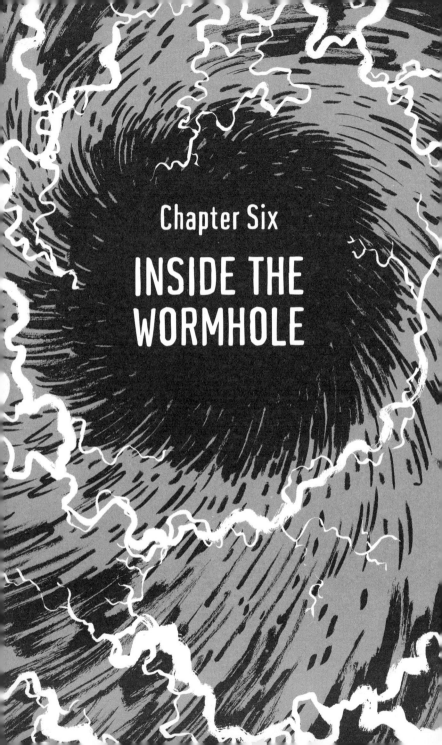

Chapter Six

INSIDE THE WORMHOLE

Treasure!

Sam clutched on to the rail of the crow's nest and held on for dear life.

The *Jolly Apollo* lurched violently to one side as the first energy wave buffeted into the ship, and Sam was nearly thrown from the crow's nest. He looked around desperately, but there was no sign of any escape route like Captain Comet had told him to look for. Like it or not, they were in the Lightning-Bolt Wormhole now!

Clinging on by his fingertips, Sam figured that the deck might be a safer place to be. He scrambled down the rigging as quickly as he could, swaying from side to side with the pitching of the ship.

By the time Sam reached the deck, the *Apollo* had been completely swallowed up by the wormhole. Bolts of lightning cracked like whips all around the ship. Sam could feel the hairs on his head lifting as the static electricity fizzed and sparked. Behind him the *Revenge* bucked and twisted as it followed the *Apollo*, dragged along by the traction beams that kept the ships linked together.

The *Apollo*'s sails slapped against the masts, which groaned with the strain.

Comet shouted something. Even though Sam was only a few paces away, he could barely hear what Comet was saying.

"WHAT?" Sam yelled back.

"HOIST THE SAILS!" Comet bellowed again. "THEY'LL SNAP THE MAST OR GET RIPPED TO SHREDS!"

"AYE AYE, CAPTAIN!" Sam shouted at the top of his voice.

Sam tapped the nearest crewmate, Romero, on the shoulder and beckoned for him to follow. Using a combination of shouts and mime Sam passed on Comet's message. Romero began pulling on the ropes that hoisted the sails while Sam tried to get other crew members to help.

Inside the wormhole the pulses of light swirled hypnotically round and round and ferocious flashes of lightning ripped this way and that. Wherever Sam looked all he could see was the spiralling walls of the wormhole, great intense

flashes of lightning and the mountainous waves of blue energy that swept the *Apollo* and the *Revenge* along like they were on the Universe's biggest roller coaster.

FIZZZZZZZZZZZZZZZZZZZZZ!

An energy wave broke across the deck, coating everything it touched in a ghostly blueish light and crackling with electricity.

"OWWW!" cried Sam as the wave hit him and gave him a static-electric shock. It felt a bit like being stabbed with lots of tiny pins.

FIZZZZZZZZZZZZZZZZZZZZZ!

Another wave broke over the *Apollo* and this time Sam and the crew jumped out of the way of the bolt of electricity, abandoning the ropes and leaving the sails to take care of themselves.

"TURN THE SHIP *TOWARDS* THE WAVES!" shouted Comet to Pegg and Legg, who were struggling with the ship's wheel. "IT'S THE ONLY WAY TO RIDE THEM!"

"WHAT?" Pegg barked back. "FERNS NIP AT THE GRAVES?"

53

"NO," snapped Legg, "CHURN AND SLIP AND BE BRAVE!"

Sam scuttled across the pitching deck to explain.

"STEER THE SHIP TOWARDS THE WAVES!" shouted Sam urgently.

"WHICH WAVES?" Legg replied.

Sam looked up and saw the blue pulses of energy were coming from all directions – it was like sailing the ship through a washing machine.

"HAVING THE *REVENGE* HANGING ON TO US ISN'T HELPING," shouted Pegg as he battled with the wheel. "WE SET OFF IN ONE DIRECTION AND THEY GET PULLED IN ANOTHER. SOMETHING'S GOING TO GIVE SOON, AND I RECKON IT'LL BE THIS OLD TUB THAT FALLS APART FIRST!"

Sam looked back at *Gravity's Revenge*, still attached by the traction beams, and could see Black-Hole Beard bellowing orders and his crew running around frantically. The huge Minocerous first mate, Yarr, was struggling at the wheel as

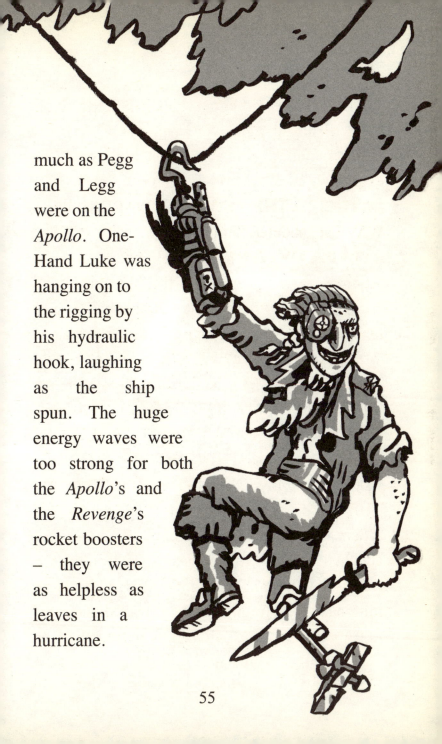

much as Pegg and Legg were on the *Apollo*. One-Hand Luke was hanging on to the rigging by his hydraulic hook, laughing as the ship spun. The huge energy waves were too strong for both the *Apollo*'s and the *Revenge*'s rocket boosters – they were as helpless as leaves in a hurricane.

The two ships were deep in the wormhole now. The solar winds were howling past them, as they were sucked in by the wormhole's gravitational pull, and combining with the energy waves to make the ride even choppier. Sam clung on as the ship pitched and shook.

Everything loose on deck was being blown overboard.

A huge energy wave swamped the *Apollo*'s deck.

"OWWWWW!" everyone shouted as they were given a static-electric shock.

"WHOSE STUPID IDEA WAS THIS?" shouted Comet as his moustache stood on end like an electrocuted Hawkinseon Hair-slug.

Before anyone could answer, the *Apollo* lurched up the side of another gigantic wave then plunged down the other side. It was so steep it was like sailing down the side of a cliff. Suddenly the air around them turned bright white and there was a huge *CRACK* as the biggest flash of lightning Sam had ever seen streaked past them – and smashed straight into the *Revenge*!

For a moment the spaceship glowed with a fierce, bright white light. Then the lightning flash was gone and the *Revenge* went completely dark. There was a deadly silence from their engines, and there wasn't a booster flare to be seen.

"WHAT'S HAPPENED?" cried Sam.

"THEY'VE LOST POWER," shouted Comet in reply. "THAT LIGHTNING

BOLT MUST HAVE BLOWN THEIR CIRCUITS."

"WILL THEY BE OK?" asked Sam.

"NO! THEIR ATOMIC STABILISERS WILL

BE DOWN. THAT'S WHAT KEEPS THE SHIP UPRIGHT!" Legg shouted back. "THEY'RE A DEAD SHIP SAILING!"

The *Revenge* was already leaning awkwardly to one side.

"AS LONG AS—" Comet started to yell, then trailed off as the noise of the wind and lightning died down slightly. He cleared his throat. "As long as the traction beams are still attached, they'll be all right..." he finished doubtfully.

"LOOK!" shouted Sam. The laser-traction beams linking the *Apollo* and the *Revenge* were beginning to flicker. "They're starting to go out!"

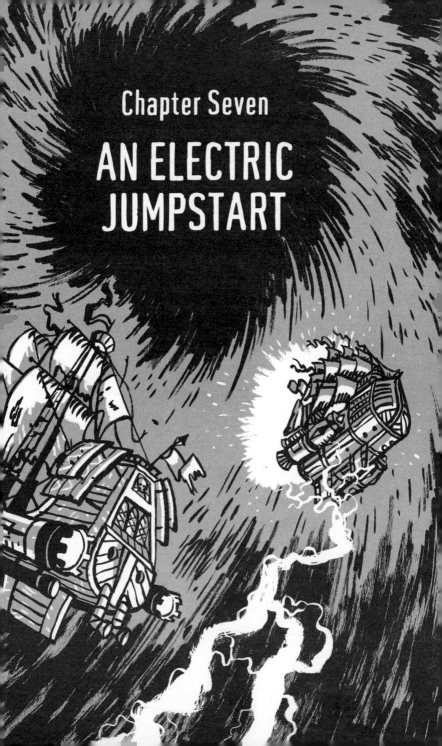

Sam could hardly bear to watch. The only thing that was standing between the *Gravity's Revenge* and destruction were the six laser-traction beams that linked Black-Hole Beard's ship to the *Apollo* – and now they were beginning to fail. The beams were flickering and flashing, losing the bright intensity of their colour.

"Looks like the traction-beam generator has been damaged too!" Legg guessed.

"Excellent!" Comet replied. "Pegg, Legg, full speed ahead. We should be able to break free if those beams are underpowered."

"No!" shouted Sam.

"Excuse me?" said Comet.

"I mean, no, *Captain*," said Sam.

"That's better— Hold on, what do you mean, *no*? I give the orders around here!" said Comet, waving his arms around wildly.

"You can't just abandon the *Revenge*!" cried Sam. "You can't just order us to fly off!"

"I can and I did," smiled Comet.

"But they'll be torn to pieces in this wormhole!"

protested Sam.

"And the problem is…? That *is* Black-Hole Beard, you know," said Comet.

"But … but…" Sam was at a loss for words. True, it was Black-Hole Beard, but leaving him to certain doom still felt wrong.

"They've lost one of the beams, Captain!" shouted Pegg. "No, make that two. Shall I fire up the engines?"

Sam had an idea.

"But what about the Pirate's Code?" he said.

"What?" Comet paused, then flipped up his eye patches to stare at everyone with all three of his eyes.

"Surely the Code says you can't abandon a ship in distress?" Sam said.

"Ignore him, Captain," shouted Pegg. "Black-Hole Beard doesn't live by the Code, so why should we?"

"The Code is the Code," said Legg. "It doesn't matter who it is."

Comet looked torn. "Yes, but the Code

isn't really a strict set of rules, it's more like *guidelines...*" he said.

"Guidelines!" said Sam disgustedly. "That's the sort of thing Black-Hole Beard would say."

Comet looked shamefaced. "Yes, you're right," he muttered, embarrassed. "I don't know what came over me. Pegg, Legg, ignore that order. Keep the *Apollo* on as straight a course as possible and maintain our speed."

"That's not going to be easy," grumbled Pegg. "It was bad enough trying to fly when they had power; now it's like doing it with a giant gravity anchor swinging round behind us."

As if to prove the point, the *Revenge* was buffeted by an energy wave and started to spin. The *Jolly Apollo* was pulled round after it so fast that the ship's wheel spun out of control.

Pegg and Legg grabbed it, but it wasn't until Sam clutched on as well, putting all his weight on the wheel, that the ship was back under control. The roller-coaster ride had just got a whole lot worse.

Treasure!

"Another one of those could knock us into a lightning storm and that would be the end of all of us!" said Legg.

"Captain, we've got to do something about the *Revenge*!" said Pegg.

"That's it!" said Sam.

"Oh, good." Pegg and Legg high-fived. "I knew you'd see sense about the Code. I'll increase the power, Cap'n – we're going to break free."

"*No*. There's a way of restarting the *Revenge*!" said Sam.

"At least, I think there is. If the lightning knocked the power out, maybe it can kick-start it back again."

"Well, I suppose…" said Comet doubtfully.

"If we fly over to that side of the wormhole we should hit that storm over there," Sam continued, pointing at a dark cluster of energy waves, where lightning was sizzling. "There's enough energy over there to power fifty ships! All we need to do is channel the lightning into the *Gravity's Revenge*."

"We're going to fly *into* a lightning storm?" Pegg shook his head in disbelief.

"And take the *Apollo* on a loop-the-loop?" Comet stuttered. "Are you mad? There's no way the old girl can handle that!"

"Has anyone got a better idea?" Sam asked. The rest of the crew muttered and stared at their feet. "Come on!" Sam said enthusiastically. "What have we got to lose?"

"Our lives, our ship, our breakfasts…" Comet started.

Treasure!

"*Captain...*" pleaded Sam.

"Oh, all right then," said Comet. "But it's not like Black-Hole Beard is even going to be grateful! Pegg, Legg, steer us to the side of the wormhole. We're heading for that storm."

Riding the crest of an energy wave, the *Apollo* changed direction and plunged towards the curved wall of the wormhole. The waves sparked and spat as the *Apollo* charged headlong up the side of the blistering energy wall.

"Hold on tight, me hearties. We're in for a choppy ride," shouted Comet over the din.

With a great whoosh the *Apollo* hit the wall of the wormhole and shot up the great fizzing curve, dragging the *Revenge* behind it. Great flashes and sparks erupted from the hulls of the ships as they sped up the side of the wormhole, the pulsing energy rattling the *Apollo* like a meteoroid in a can. Above them, dark clouds boiled and lightning licked angrily at the air.

"What happens if *we* get hit by one of those lightning bolts?" asked Zlit, clinging to the rigging with both claws.

Comet suddenly looked panicked. "I knew there was a good reason not to do this!" he wailed.

Too late now, thought Sam.

He looked back to see how the *Revenge* was doing, just in time to see the third and then fourth traction beams flicker out. Now there were only two left, and they were fading fast. The *Apollo* dragged the *Revenge* closer and closer to the crackling lightning storm.

As the ships were swept round the wormhole they tilted more and more.

"HOLD ON, ME HEARTIES!" Comet bellowed as the ship twisted and turned. Sam looked round desperately for something to grab hold of. Pegg and Legg were tying themselves to the ship's wheel, Romero had clamped himself to a mast, and Captain Comet was trying to stuff himself into the mouth of a laser cannon. The whole ship tilted as the energy waves carried them up the side of the wormhole.

Sam was out of time. He quickly grabbed the

edge of the deck rail. The *Jolly Apollo* twisted again, turning so much that Sam's feet were now hanging in mid-air.

The *Apollo* neared the top of the wormhole, but Sam could feel his hands beginning to slip. He held on as tight as he could, but it was no use, his fingers were slipping.

"NOOOOOOOOO!" cried Sam as his grip gave way and he dropped into the twirling vortex of the wormhole.

SLAP! A tentacle caught him around the waist! Barney was swinging from the front mast, holding another three pirates in his tentacles. One, Jonjarama, seemed to be quite enjoying himself and gave Sam a thumbs-up. Barney gave him a wink.

CRRRAACCCCCKKKK!

A huge flash of lightning scorched past the *Apollo*.

PAZZZAAAAPPPPPPP!

It smashed into the traction beams and zapped along

SPACE PIRATES

to the *Gravity's Revenge*. Immediately their rocket boosters fired up again. There was a great shower of sparks as power surged back into the *Revenge*, then the traction beams exploded in a flash of neon light as the sudden electrical hit overwhelmed the machinery. The blast sent the *Revenge* spiralling away down the wormhole.

"It worked!" shouted Sam. "And we're free!"

"Ha! Those planet-lubbers can look after themselves now!" crowed Comet, climbing out from the cannon. "Full speed ahead!"

The *Jolly Apollo* blasted along, riding the waves much more easily without the other ship dragging behind it. There were fewer energy waves in this section so the ride was much smoother and the noise wasn't as loud – much to everyone's relief. At the far end of the wormhole was the darkness of space and it was getting nearer by the second.

"The dark at the end of the tunnel!" said Comet, peering through his telescope at the light. "We'll be there in no time now, me hearties!"

The crew cheered and the rocket boosters

roared. Sam smiled so much that his face ached. He couldn't quite believe it; after all this time, and against all the odds, he was actually going to get to Planet X to rescue his parents.

With a *WHOOSH* the *Apollo* shot out from the Lightning-Bolt Wormhole. As they cleared the mist around the mouth of the wormhole they could see it… Directly ahead of them, in the middle of deep, black space, was the magnificent, legendary, beautiful Planet X!

Chapter Eight
PLANET X

Treasure!

It was everything the legends said it was; a great glowing, golden ball that gleamed and shone like a beacon. A planet made of solid gold!

For a while the pirates stared in awestruck silence. Sam could hardly believe it – they had done it! In their battered old spaceship they had managed to do what no other pirate crew had done – they had ridden the lightning and found Planet X!

"Rich!" Comet crowed. "I'm going to be rich! And famous! I'm going to be the most famous pirate in the Universe! Rich *and* famous!" He fired his laser pistol into the air in celebration.

"Hey! Careful down there!" shouted Vulpus from the crow's nest. "That nearly took my tail off!"

"What are you going to buy with your share of the treasure?" Romero asked Zlit.

"A ginormous heated grum pool!" Zlit replied.

"I'm going to get a diamond-encrusted bowling ball," said Romero. "No wait, a diamond-encrusted bowling *alley*!"

"Think of all the food we'll be able to buy!" said Piole in wide-eyed, drooling-mouthed anticipation. "Zeeper burgers, Antovian roasted booglers, jum-jum pancakes, jellied spim-spams, scottle cakes, wispy angel chimneys – and that's just for starters!"

Pegg and Legg were arguing about what they would spend the money on.

"I'm going to hire a chef," said Barney, to the stunned amazement of the crew.

"How about you, Sam?" the Kracken asked.

Sam didn't reply. A horrible thought had taken over his brain.

"What's wrong, Sam? You look worried."

"What if my parents aren't here?" Sam gulped. "What if they've been picked up by someone else? What if… What if they're not alive?"

Barney put a comforting tentacle on Sam's shoulder.

"Sorry, Sam, I keep forgetting that Planet X means more to you than the treasure. I'm sure they're going to be fine. Their spaceship had emergency provisions, and your mother was well enough to draw a map and write you a message. Just you wait and see, soon you'll be giving them the best surprise of their lives!"

Sam smiled. He certainly hoped Barney was right.

The excitement on board the *Apollo* was almost unbearable as the spaceship drew closer to Planet X. Soon it was breaching the outer layers of the planet's atmosphere. Although the *Apollo* was buffeted this way and that as it descended down to the planet's surface, it was nothing compared to the nightmare of the Lightning-Bolt Wormhole.

"Turn the rocket boosters off and fire the reverse thrusters," ordered Comet as the golden surface rushed towards them.

"Aye aye, sir," said Legg.

The rocket boosters went off, but nothing else came on.

"Reverse thrusters, p-please, Pegg and Legg," said Comet, a small note of desperation in his voice.

"We're trying!" said Pegg. "But the button isn't working. Again."

Below them the ground was approaching at a frightening speed.

"Batten down the hatches. This might be a bumpy landing!" shouted Comet.

Might be a bumpy landing? thought Sam incredulously. *They're* always *bumpy landings!*

Seconds later the *Apollo* was screeching across the surface of the planet, bouncing and bumping over lumps and rocks. With a final CRUNCH it stopped, nose first, in a wide ditch. A great cloud of dust rose up and settled over the ship.

"Well, that wasn't so bad," said Comet, dusting himself down and looking round the ship, which seemed to be in one piece. "Nothing valuable damaged!"

"He must have landed on his head," snorted Pegg.

"Right me hearties, it's time to go for gold!"

The pirates rushed for the ship's rails, but Sam stayed sitting on the deck. Something wasn't right. The dust that had been thrown up by the crash – it was dirt.

"Erm, Captain," he said, but it was too late; the pirates had already leapt over the side. Immediately he could hear their disappointed cries.

Sam jumped over the ship's rail and joined the rest of the crew.

"What happened to all the gold?" wailed Comet, holding two handfuls of dirt.

"It's up there," said Vulpus, pointing to the golden-coloured sky.

"It's just an illusion made by the planet's atmosphere!" Comet cried.

"So the legend was wrong," sobbed Jonjarama.

Sam wasn't listening though. All he could think about was his parents. He raced up the nearest hill and frantically began to look around. Immediately he saw a metallic glint, not far below him. There was a large purple-coloured pool … and next to it was a spaceship. In front of the ship was a small, neatly tended garden. He couldn't believe it! Surely there were only two people who would make a garden next to a space-wreck – space

Treasure!

scientists who studied alien plant-life. Space scientists like his parents!

"Dad! Mum!" he yelled as he charged down the hill, his feet sending up great clouds of dust.

Out from the spaceship came two figures: one, a woman, in a tattered spacesuit; the other, a man, with a matching spacesuit and a bushy beard. They peered at the boy running towards them for a moment.

"Sam!" they shouted, and began running towards their son.

They met halfway in the biggest, and quite possibly the best, hug imaginable.

Chapter Nine

CASTOR AND STELLA STARBUCK

Treasure!

Eventually Sam and his parents pulled themselves apart.

"Nice beard, Dad," grinned Sam.

"Never mind the beard – how did you get here?" said his dad, looking at him in amazement.

"We were hoping that Interstellar Rescue was going to come, but when they didn't show we thought we were stuck here forever," his mother said. "We're so happy to see you!"

"I got the homing beacon with the map in it," explained Sam, "but it hit the satellite aerial on the house when it landed and broke it. I couldn't get in touch with anybody."

"So how did you get here?" asked his dad.

Sam was about to explain when Captain Comet and his crew appeared over the brow of the hill.

"SPACE PIRATES!" shouted Sam's dad. "Quick, Sam, get into the ship with your mother and lock the door. I'll try and hold them off with … with … erm," He looked round for something that could be used as a weapon. All he could find was a long-stemmed flower from the garden.

Sam just laughed.

"Don't worry, Dad, it's only Captain Comet – I'm part of his crew."

"You're a *space pirate*?" asked his mother.

"I stowed away on their ship," Sam explained. "It was the only way I could get off P-Sezov 8 to try and get help. When they found me I told them about the map…"

"You showed *space pirates* the map! Was that wise?" asked his dad.

"I'm here, aren't I?" Sam said smiling. "And they're not your *usual* pirates! Come and see for yourself."

Comet and his crew appeared by the spaceship. Comet swept off his tricorn hat and bowed extravagantly.

"Mr and Mrs Starbuck, I presume," he said. "May I introduce myself: I am Captain Joseph Hercules Invictus Comet, of the pirate spaceship the *Jolly Apollo*, and this is my crew. Do not worry; we mean you no harm. Rather, we have come to rescue you. Ooh, a flower. For me?

82

Thank you!"

He took the flower from Sam's dad and gave it a sniff.

"Ah, delightful! Now, I take it that is your ship?" Comet continued.

"Erm, yes," Sam's dad replied. He seemed to be struggling a bit with this unusual and surprising turn of events. "I think we've damaged the auto-sensors, and the reverse thrusters are a bit mangled."

"Right-ho, me hearty, we can get that fixed – we have some experience of repairing ships. Romero, Zlit, see what you can do about getting that vessel up in the air again."

"Aye aye, Cap'n," the pirates replied.

"Oh, thank you. I'll show you the damage," said Sam's dad.

"I don't know how to repay you." Sam's mum smiled.

"Nonsense, madam. Your son has been so much help to us that we are simply returning the favour," said Comet.

"Aye, that and the hope of getting rich by finding Planet X – but that plan didn't work," grumbled Pegg.

"Yes..." said Comet. He leaned in close to Sam's mum. "This is definitely Planet X, isn't it?

Treasure!

It's just we were led to believe that it was made of gold, islands of rubies … that sort of thing."

Stella Starbuck hugged Sam close. "Yes, this *is* Planet X," she smiled. "And since you've come all this way to rescue us, there's something I think you should see."

She led everyone past the crash site to the edge of the purple pool. Sam could hear a gentle thundering noise. At one side of the pool was a waterfall that tumbled and foamed into a large pool of the purple water below. Sam's mum started to climb down the rocks by the side of the waterfall. Sam and the pirates followed.

"Where does this take us, Mum?" asked Sam.

"You'll see," she smiled.

The rock face was steep and tricky to climb down, but eventually they all reached the bottom safely. The pool spread into a huge cavern that echoed to the sound of dripping water. Inside was a great underground lake, and above it large stalactites, easily as long as the main mast on the *Apollo*, hung like the spires of upside-down

churches – but that wasn't what grabbed everyone's attention.

"Mum, are those *rubies*?" Sam asked, pointing to the huge red stones glinting from the cavern walls.

"They are," she replied.

"Well, blow me down with a hoob feather," said Comet. "They're enormous!"

"And there are hundreds of them," said Sam.

"Thousands," gasped Legg and Pegg together.

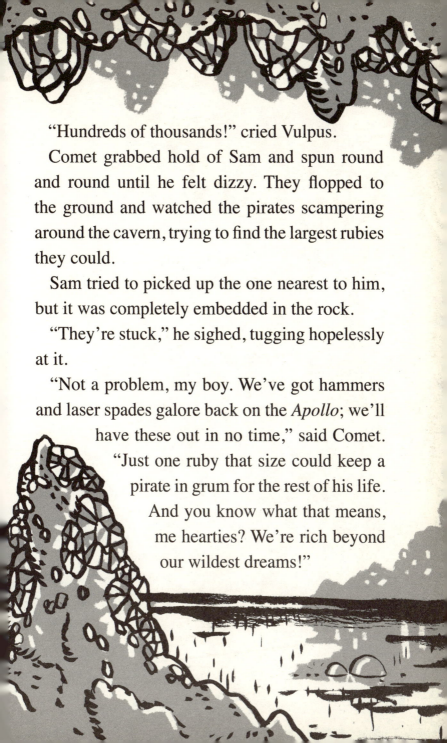

"Hundreds of thousands!" cried Vulpus.

Comet grabbed hold of Sam and spun round and round until he felt dizzy. They flopped to the ground and watched the pirates scampering around the cavern, trying to find the largest rubies they could.

Sam tried to picked up the one nearest to him, but it was completely embedded in the rock.

"They're stuck," he sighed, tugging hopelessly at it.

"Not a problem, my boy. We've got hammers and laser spades galore back on the *Apollo*; we'll have these out in no time," said Comet. "Just one ruby that size could keep a pirate in grum for the rest of his life. And you know what that means, me hearties? We're rich beyond our wildest dreams!"

Chapter Ten
DWARFSTAR'S CHEST

Treasure!

"I don't know about anyone else," said Barney, slapping Sam playfully on the back, "but being rich has made me really thirsty. I'm going for a drink. Bet that purple water tastes like maroonberries!"

"Barney, I'm not sure that's a good idea; you don't know what's in it," Sam replied. "Mum, is this water OK to drink?"

"NO!" his mum cried. "Stop him!"

Sam dived at Barney, grabbing his tentacles in a rugby tackle.

"Hey, what's the big idea!" shouted Barney.

"That water's highly acidic. Look at that poor chap," Sam's mum explained.

Lying by the edge of the pool was a badly dissolved skeleton with a shiny metal key on a chain draped round its neck.

"Whoa," said Sam.

He carefully removed the key and chain from the skeleton. The key was a bright silvery-white colour with a golden skull on the flattened end. The skull had two blood-red gems for eyes and

diamonds for teeth.

"Why didn't this dissolve, like the bones?" Sam asked, putting the chain around his neck.

"Because it's made of quantillium," said Comet in a strange voice.

"Quantillium? I've never heard of it," said Sam's mum.

"It's the rarest, strongest material in the Universe," said Comet, his eyes wide open. "And if I'm right, there should be a symbol on the key."

"There is: a golden skull with red eyes and what looks like—"

"Diamonds for teeth," Comet continued.

Comet leaned in closely to look at the key. His hands were shaking and beads of sweat were forming on his brow. Sam had never seen him like this before – Comet looked nervous, but a really, really excited kind of nervous. He stared for a few seconds, clapped his hands together, whooped with joy and did an excited dance around the edge of the lake.

"Pegg, Legg, call the crew," he shouted. "I've

got news! Amazing news! STUPENDOUS news!"

"What's up?" asked Sam.

"What's up?" Comet repeated. "EVERYTHING! That there key, that wonderful key you're holding, is only the key to Dwarfstar's chest!"

Comet waited for a reaction, but Sam and his mother didn't have a clue what he was talking about.

"Planet-lubbers," sighed Comet under his breath. "Right, me hearties, ready yourselves for a tale and a half. Dwarfstar was the meanest, most successful pirate in the history of piracy. He disappeared years ago, leaving his treasure chest. The Pirate Council have been guarding it ever since. They have decreed that whoever finds the key, gets the chest!"

"Why doesn't someone just break into the chest?" asked Sam.

"It's against the Pirate's Code!" said Comet, horrified.

Sam shook his head; he would never understand the Code.

"Besides, it's made from quantillium, so no one *can* get in. But now we've got the key!" crowed Comet, "we're going to be the most famous pirates in the galaxy!"

"And the richest!" cheered Sam.

"This calls for a celebration!" Comet yelled. "Back to the *Apollo*, boys. The grum's on me!"

The happy pirates started clambering back up the rocks by the waterfall.

"After you, madam." Comet bowed low to Sam's mum. Stella put her arm round Sam as they followed the pirates back up the cliff.

"It's all worked out OK," she grinned as they reached the top. "You're safe, the pirates are rich, and your father and I have been rescued."

"Let's not be hasty there, me deary," said a deep, gruff voice. A rough hand grabbed Sam's mum and she screamed.

Sam scrambled after his mum quickly, then froze as he reached the top. Black-Hole Beard

Treasure!

was standing there with a laser cutlass held to his mum's neck. His clothes looked slightly blackened and charred from the lightning strike.

Behind him, Goldstar, Yarr, One-Hand Luke and the rest of the *Revenge*'s crew had surrounded Sam's dad, Barney, Zlit, Romero and the other pirates from the *Jolly Apollo*.

"What's wrong, Sam?" puffed Comet as he reached the top. "Oh, shiver me timbers – it's him!"

"Ahoy there, Joseph," said Black-Hole Beard. "Surprised to see me?"

"I take it this *isn't* one of your friends, Sam?" gulped Sam's mother.

"You've guessed right there, me lass!" Black-Hole Beard gave a cruel smile. "Me and the *Apollo* have some unfinished business to attend to. Especially seeing as how they tried to get us killed in that there wormhole."

"Killed!" Sam protested. "We saved your lives!"

"It's true," Comet added. "We got the *Revenge* running again."

"Ha!" barked Black-Hole Beard, stroking his beard menacingly. "Mebbe you did. But ye

also got us electrocuted on purpose … and now it seems like Planet X is as useless as you are, Comet. You've led us on a wild gold chase…"

Black-Hole Beard's voice trailed away – instead he was staring at the key around Sam's neck.

"Well, well, well, me hearty, what have you got there?"

"That? Oh, that's nothing," said Comet, standing in front of Sam.

"CAWR! Liar! Liar! Pants on fire!" cawed Baggot.

"Yes, me pretty, I reckons he is," muttered Black-Hole Beard. "Now, Joseph, that wouldn't be Dwarfstar's key, would it? A skull with two gems the colour of a red dwarf? I'd recognise that symbol anywhere!"

Black-Hole Beard edged closer with a menacing glint in his eye, brushing past Comet. Sam stepped back. His heels were hanging over the edge of the cliff and the purple lake was fizzing menacingly below him.

"Now, let's not do anything stupid, me boy," said Black-Hole Beard in his most wheedling voice. "Just pass the key over here and I'll let your parents go."

"Let them go first," said Sam, pulling the key over his head and clutching it tightly in his fist.

"No, no, no, me hearty, that's not going to happen," said Black-Hole Beard, edging ever nearer, dragging Sam's mum with him.

Sam shuffled back a little more until he was really teetering on the edge. He stared round desperately, trying to think of what to do.

Comet was creeping around behind Black-Hole Beard. As Sam watched, Comet widened his eyes and pointed to himself. Sam suddenly knew what Comet wanted him to do.

"OK then," Sam said to Black-Hole Beard. "Both at the same time – agreed?"

"Aye," grunted Black-Hole Beard.

"Right, on my count of three. One … two … THREE!"

Sam threw the key up into the air over Black-

Treasure!

Hole Beard's head, towards Captain Comet. Black-Hole Beard pushed Sam's mother roughly to one side as he leapt up for it. The key glinted as it arced through the air. Comet jumped at the same time and Sam lunged towards his mum, but his back foot slipped. Sam wobbled, arms windmilling frantically as he tried to keep his balance.

"Arrrgggghhhh!" he cried as he tumbled over the edge.

Chapter Eleven

COMET'S CHOICE

Treasure!

Desperately, Sam threw out a hand as he fell and grabbed at a bunch of grassy reeds. Legs kicking in the air, he managed to haul himself up, bracing his elbows on the edge, struggling to get himself back on solid ground. A shower of rocks cascaded down the cliff and bounced into the deadly water below, where they fizzed loudly as they dissolved.

Sam glanced up and saw his mum lying on the ground. His dad, Barney and the other pirates were fighting the crew of *Gravity's Revenge* to try and reach Sam, but it didn't look like they were winning. Dwarfstar's key had landed on the ground between Comet and Black-Hole Beard and both pirates were dashing towards it greedily.

"Help!" cried Sam. "I'm slipping!"

There was an awful sound of ripping vegetation as Sam fell further down the rock face. He glanced down and saw more stones cascade into the water. Sam scrabbled at the grass, but there was nothing he could do. "Help!" he yelled again desperately. But it was too late. The grass came away in his hand, and Sam plunged down the cliff.

Suddenly a pair of hands shot over the edge and grabbed his wrists. Sam dangled in mid-air as he looked up at his saviour – Captain Comet!

"Avast there, me hearty!" said Comet. "Let's get you upright and shipshape."

Sam was stunned. He was sure Comet had been going for Dwarfstar's key! Barney and the crew appeared at the edge of the cliff, and Barney easily lifted the pair of them, using his tentacles to haul

them back up to safety, where they fell in an unceremonious heap. His dad was close by, taking care of Sam's mum. In the distance Black-Hole Beard and his crew were speeding back to the *Revenge*, cheering and whooping all the way.

"What happened?" asked Sam.

"Well, you slipped and I caught you," said Comet, dusting himself down.

"But how did Black-Hole Beard get the key?"

"No real choice," said Comet with a shrug. "It was you or the key. You never leave a crewmate behind. It's the—"

"Pirate's Code?" said Sam.

"Aye, me hearty, the Pirate's Code," smiled Comet.

"But Dwarfstar's treasure?" said Sam.

"Aye, Black-Hole Beard will be unbearable now," said Comet, "but I couldn't lose my cabin boy."

"Well, not another one," muttered Pegg.

"And look on the bright side, you're still rich," said Sam's mum, rubbing a lump on the side of her head.

"Indeed, my lady," said Comet. "Who can put a price on friendship?"

"No, I mean there's still the rubies," said Sam's mum.

"Well, blow down me main braces, I'd completely forgotten about them, what with all the fuss and all!" said Comet. "Avast, me hearties! There's treasure to load!"

Chapter Twelve

A SAD GOODBYE

Loading the *Jolly Apollo* with all the rubies took a long time, but no one was complaining. In fact, everyone was so busy getting the job done that they didn't even stop to celebrate with a tankard of grum. Although the crew were happy, Sam could see that something was still bothering Captain Comet.

"What's wrong, Captain?" he asked.

"I almost had it," he muttered sadly. "The key to Dwarfstar's treasure, the greatest pirate horde ever collected, in my hands. It could have been mine…"

"And you gave it up to Black-Hole Beard to save me," said Sam.

"Oh, it was worth it, but I'd feel a lot happier if I had it back," Captain Comet answered.

Suddenly Comet's face lit up and his moustache pinged out at each side of his face.

"That's it!" he declared. "We'll go and get it back!"

"Get it back – from Black-Hole Beard?" said Sam.

"We've tricked him before and we can trick him again!" said Comet. "The last thing he'll be expecting is us sneaking up on him. We'll nip in and out like space thieves in the night. What could possibly go wrong?"

Sam could think of plenty of things that could go wrong, but the chance of getting one over on Black-Hole Beard was too good an opportunity to miss. Besides, if it wasn't for him, Black-Hole Beard wouldn't have the key and the *Jolly Apollo* would be heading to claim the prize.

"OK, Captain, let's do it!" Sam cried.

Comet sprang into action, slamming his hat on to his head and pulling up his two eye-patches to show his three good eyes underneath. "Right, me hearties," he bellowed. "All aboard the *Apollo*. We've got our fortune stowed away, but now we're going to chase down those dogs on the *Revenge* and get our key back! What say you?"

The crew cheered.

"Sam," Stella called. "We're ready to go. Time to say goodbye to your friends."

His mother's voice caught him by surprise. She and his dad were standing in front of their spaceship. It looked battered and patched up, but ready to fly.

"Say goodbye?" asked Sam confusedly.

"Yes, it's time for us all to go home," his dad replied.

"But we're about to chase Black-Hole Beard," said Sam.

"Go after that evil brute? Not on your life!" said Sam's mum, looking shocked at the idea.

"But—" Sam started to complain.

"Sam, you're a schoolboy, not a pirate. You should be catching up with your lessons and

learning: not risking your life with a bunch of outlaws," said his dad. "No offence, guys," he added, waving at the pirates trooping up the plank to the *Apollo*.

Lessons? Sam thought of sitting at home with his holo-teacher droning on. It felt weird, like it was an image from someone else's life. It wasn't who Sam felt he was any more.

"Hurry along, me hearty. Look shipshape," called Captain Comet, coming back down the *Apollo*'s gangplank. "What's the hold-up?"

"I'm not allowed to come," said Sam. He felt so awful he thought he might cry.

"What? But you're my cabin boy. Is this a joke?" Comet smiled expectantly. "You tricksters!"

Sam shook his head sadly. Comet's face dropped, and his moustache sagged so much that the two ends almost touched under his chin. "But we need you!" he exclaimed.

"I'm sorry, Captain, but we think Sam really needs to be at home," Stella said, putting an arm around Sam's shoulders. "He's got school work

to catch up on and we're not sure he's really ready for exploring space like this."

The rest of the crew were gathering on board the *Jolly Apollo*. Sam looked up to see Barney, Pegg and Legg, and all his friends staring down at him sadly.

"So this is … goodbye?" said Comet.

"I'm afraid so," said Sam's dad.

Sam was too choked up to speak. Barney ran down the plank and grabbed him in an enormous, multi-tentacled hug. Then he returned to the *Apollo,* sobbing and dabbing his eyes.

"You'd better have this," said Comet, taking off his tricorn hat and plonking it on Sam's head. "Something to remember us by. We'll come and visit next time we're at the pirate port on P-Sezov 8."

Comet sniffed, shook Sam's hand and walked sadly up the plank.

"Raise the anchors, hoist the main sails," he ordered.

Sam and his parents watched as the *Jolly Apollo*

hauled herself slowly into the sky. Sam closed his eyes as the pirate ship left. It was a terrible ship – cold, draughty, and always breaking down – but Sam couldn't bear to watch it fly away.

Chapter Thirteen
THE END?

Treasure!

The Starbucks returned to their ship and fired up the engines.

"They did a great job on the repairs," said Sam's dad, trying to lighten the mood as their ship rose from the dusty surface of Planet X.

Sam was in no mood to be cheered up though. He flopped down into a seat and thought sadly about what had just happened. Although he'd only been on the *Apollo* for a short time, the crew had become the closest friends he had ever known. He could hardly begin to think of the adventures they'd be having while he was stuck in a room listening to his holo-teacher.

Sam shuffled miserably in his seat and promptly felt a sharp pain in his leg as something stabbed him. He put his hand in his pocket and pulled out a key – the key to the *Apollo*'s grum store! He'd forgotten that he'd put it in his pocket, back when Black-Hole Beard had first tried to grab on to the *Revenge* with his traction beams.

"Dad, Mum, I've still got a key from the *Apollo*," cried Sam. "It's really important to them. We have to take it back! Please, they won't have gone far."

"Oh, I'm sure they'll cope," Sam's mum replied.

"There's probably a spare," said his dad as he pointed the ship in the direction of home.

"There isn't!" said Sam. "Please, this would mean a lot to them." Sam could imagine the state the pirates would be in if they couldn't get to their grum.

His parents sighed. "All right, but we're not hanging around," said his mother.

Sam punched the air with joy. His dad reset the controls and their spaceship doubled-back

the way they'd come. Sure enough, they soon caught sight of the *Apollo's* booster trails ... but something wasn't right.

"Why is it flying like that?" asked Sam's dad as he watched the *Apollo* jerk and stutter on its way.

"They'll have forgotten to extend the stabiliser rods, they're always doing that. Or it might be the hyper-drive needs adjusting," Sam replied.

"You know how to do that?" asked Sam's mum, sounding impressed.

"Oh yeah, it's dead easy. I've done it loads of times," Sam replied.

The Starbucks' spaceship moored alongside the *Apollo* and the crew cheered when they saw Sam descending from the ladder – and cheered even louder when they saw what he'd brought with him.

"I feared another mutiny if we couldn't get the grum," said Comet, only half joking. "And I don't

113

know what's up with the old *Apollo*. She won't fly right now you're gone! I was trying to work out what was up with her when you arrived."

"What about the stabiliser rods? Or the hyper-drive?" Sam suggested.

"Of course! Why didn't I think of that?" Comet replied, slapping his forehead. "It's such a shame that Sam isn't round here now, to keep us right…"

Sam's parents felt the eyes of the crew on them.

"But his schooling…" said his dad.

Just then, Sam had an idea and felt so excited he almost yelped with joy.

"I can do my lessons here!" he cried. "The holoscreen! Professor Argon can link up with the holoscreen. It would be good for all of us. He could teach the captain navigation and Barney how to cook …"

"I'll have you know my navigational skills are first rate, but I'm sure Sam and Barney will get a lot out of it," said Comet.

"But your safety…" said Sam's mum.

"I give you my word that we'll keep him safe,"

said Comet. "After all, I gave away the greatest treasure in the Universe to rescue him, did I not?"

"Well, yes…" said Sam's mum.

"And I'd love Sam to be there on Shan-Greelah when we claim Dwarfstar's chest," added Comet. "I'll even promote him. Instead of cabin boy, he can be … er … thirty-third mate!"

"You're going to Shan-Greelah?" said Sam's dad.

"Yes, that's where the Pirate Council is based."

"Shan-Greelah, the home of meteor moss?" asked Sam's mum, suddenly very interested.

"If you mean that green stuff that sticks to everything, then yes," Comet replied.

Sam had another idea. "If you let me go I could bring you back a sample of meteor moss," he suggested.

Sam's parents looked at each other.

"Oh, let him come!" pleaded Barney.

"Yeah, let him come," said Romero.

"Let him come! Let him come!" the crew chanted.

"OK, OK," laughed Sam's dad. "But you take care of our boy!"

"And you check in with us every day," said Sam's mum to her son. "And do your lessons, and eat your greens…" But the rest of what she was saying was muffled, as Sam gave her the biggest hug of her life.

The Starbucks were seen back on to their ship with much cheering, and were soon on their way back home. Sam and Comet watched them until their ship disappeared from sight. Sam felt odd watching them go again, especially having spent so long looking for them, but he was happy knowing that they were safe. And, best of all, he could stay with his friends on the *Jolly Apollo*!

"So, thirty-third mate, eh?" Sam said happily.

"Yes, but don't get too big for your boots," Comet told him. "There are only thirty-three crew members."

Sam laughed. "You might need this back," he said, handing Comet his hat.

"Ah yes, thank you, Sam." Comet settled the

Treasure!

tricorn hat on his head and addressed the crew.

"Right, me hearties, prepare to sail. We've got adventures to have and treasure to find! Full speed after *Gravity's Revenge*!"

"Aye aye, Captain," Sam grinned. "Aye aye!"

Meet
THE GRUNTS!

Oh, go on.
They're not that bad.
No, actually, they ARE.
Maybe worse, even...

Just watch out
for the bees!

Read all about their
ridiculous antics in: